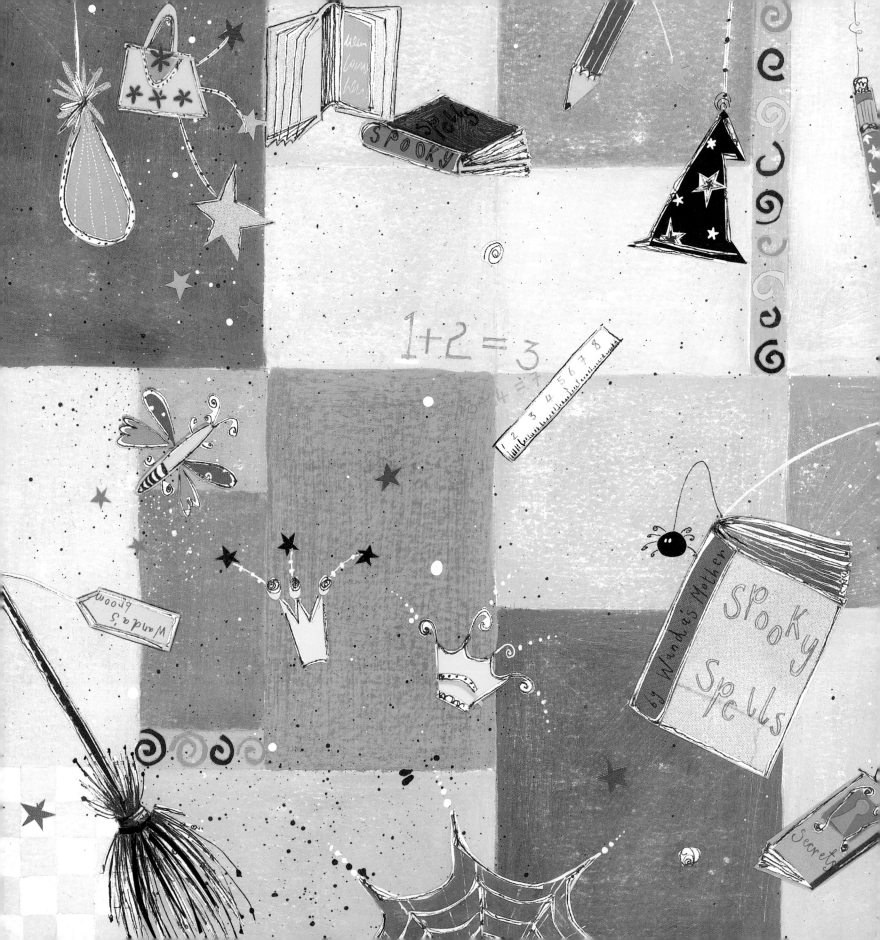

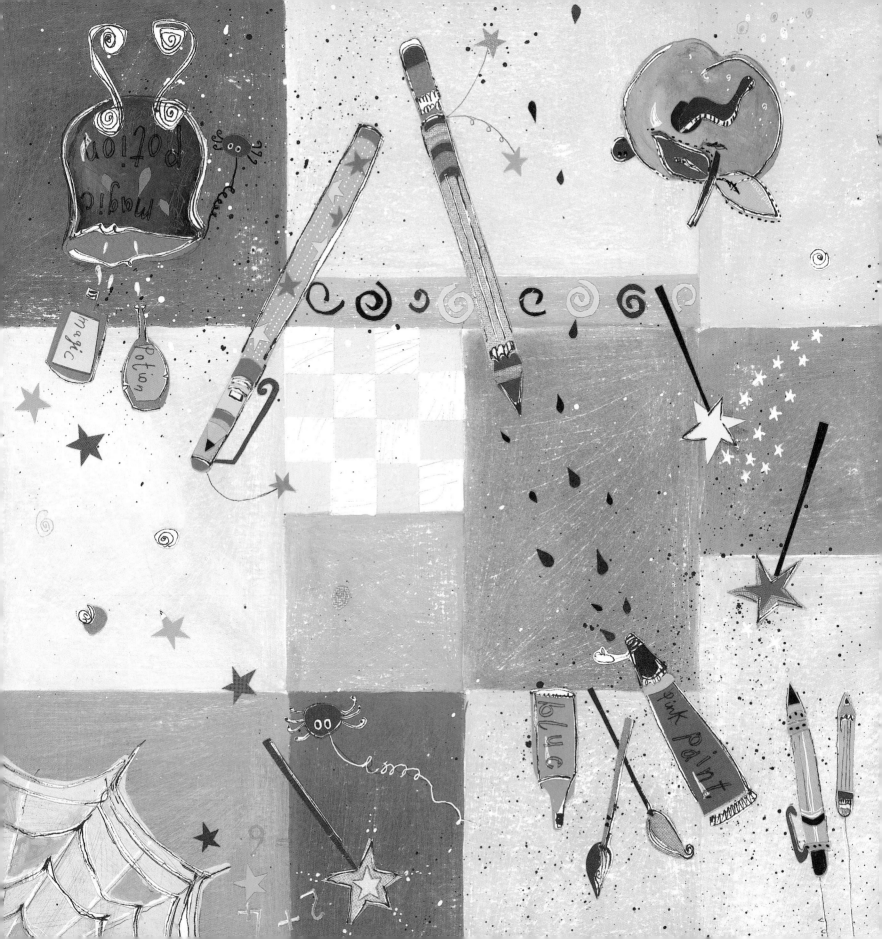

Wanda's First Day

by
Mark Sperring

illustrated by
Kate & Liz Pope

SCHOLASTIC INC.

New York Toronto London Auckland Sydney
Mexico City New Delhi Hong Kong Buenos Aires

Wanda's mom packed a delicious lunch for her first day of school. There were octopus sandwiches and lizard's breath lemonade and really tasty frogs' eggs and rat's tail yogurt.

"Remember to be wicked at school!" Wanda's mom called as she waved good-bye. "But not *too* wicked."

"I'll try," Wanda promised.

As Wanda flew to school she felt a little nervous. Half of her wanted to stay at home with her mom, but the other half thought it might be fun to go to school and make lots of new friends.

But when Wanda got to school and sat at her desk,
she looked around and couldn't help feeling
that something wasn't quite right.

"Excuse me, Miss Dewdrop," Wanda said.

"What's wrong, dear?" her teacher asked.

Wanda whispered in Miss Dewdrop's ear, "I don't think I'm supposed to be here. I think there's been some mistake."

"Nonsense," said Miss Dewdrop. "Everyone feels a bit like that on their first day of school."

But everyone looked so different from Wanda.
And Wanda looked so different from everyone else.

During recess, someone asked Wanda where her wand was.
She felt a little silly. Wanda only had a broomstick.

play area

And when someone asked Wanda where her wings were,
she drank some magic potion from her bag and .....

KABOOM!

Wanda's wings & things

But even her wings didn't look quite the same as the other girls'.

Later, in class, Wanda pulled her pet, Frieda, from her pocket to show her new friend, Tulip Fluffyglow.

But Miss Dewdrop said pets were
best left at home.

At lunchtime, Wanda shared some food with a girl named Willow Peachbreath. "These are yummy!" said Wanda, trying one of Willow's sandwiches and offering Willow one of her own.

Lizard breat Lemon

That afternoon the students made flowers grow from seeds.
But Wanda's flower was different.

Miss Dewdrop said, "Wanda dear, can you get your plant to put me down?"

Just before the end of the day, Wanda looked out of the window and saw some students from another school go by.

tulip's

by flutter

$1+3=4$

$2+1=3$

How to make lovely flowers grow

Pink Paint

"Miss Dewdrop?" Wanda said. "Are you sure I'm at the right school?"

Miss Dewdrop thought perhaps Wanda hadn't enjoyed herself. "Didn't you like your first day?" the teacher asked.

Wanda thought about the delicious food she'd eaten and the plant that she'd grown. "Yes, I did," Wanda said.

"And have you met some nice new friends?" Miss Dewdrop asked.

Wanda thought about Tulip Fluffyglow and Willow Peachbreath. "Well, yes, I suppose I have!" Wanda said, smiling.

"Perhaps you don't like me?" Miss Dewdrop asked.
Wanda blushed and said she thought Miss Dewdrop was a fine teacher.
"Well then," said Miss Dewdrop, "you're definitely at the right school,
and we shall all look forward to seeing you tomorrow."

1 2 3

School be

Miss
Dewdrop's
School

fairy flowers

And that night, snuggled up in bed, Wanda decided that the next day she would take something

extra nice and extra special to Miss Dewdrop.

4 Mum & 4 Dad – M.S.

For Mum and Dad with love –The Pope Twins

ISBN 0-439-67907-9

Text copyright © 2004 by Mark Sperring
Illustrations copyright © 2004 by Liz and Kate Pope

First published in the United Kingdom in 2004 by The Chicken House,
2 Palmer Street, Frome, Somerset, BA 11 1DS.
Email: chickenhouse@doublecluck.com.

All rights reserved. Published by Scholastic Inc., by arrangement with The Chicken House. SCHOLASTIC and associated logos are trademarks and/or registered trademarks of Scholastic Inc. THE CHICKEN HOUSE is a registered trademark of Chicken House Publishing, Limited.

10 9 8 7 6 5 4 3 2 1   04 05 06 07 08

Printed in Singapore 46
First American paperback edition, September 2004
Designed by Ian Butterworth